▪▪

The authors have created short stories that appeal to their own background knowledge; they assume no responsibility for errors, inaccuracies, omissions or any inconsistency herein. Any slights of people or organizations are unintentional. In order to reflect 5th graders' writing abilities, editing and revisions have been guided, but not perfected by teachers. Readers should consult an attorney or accountant for specific application to their individual publishing ventures.

Quixote Press

Bruce Carlson
Wever, Iowa 52658

Printed
in the
U.S.A.

5th Grade Authors

Bryson Abbey
Lakin Abbey
Rhyan Amrine
Chris Andries
Ceairra Barker
Alexa Bell-Randolph
Lexy Bergthold
Allison Berryhill
Parth Bhoja
Jayme Bigger
William Bihn
Austen Brand
Shawn Carrell
Gillian Cates
Nicole Crespo
Frank Davis
Megan Derr
Jessica Fitzgerald
Courtney Ford
Jon Geoffrion
Hanna Goebel
Abbigale Gordy
Adrian Gomez

Lexi Gonzales
Shylynn Hart
Brian Hayes
Kelsey Heidbreder
Steven Hinojosa
Tanner Hocker
Meagan Hoenig
Shelby Kemper
Tyler Landrum
Savannah Lorton
Jennifer Markey
Kristen Meierotto
Dajada Meredith
David Nagel
Hannah Puls
Angel Richardson
Kaytlyn Roberts
Dakota Salerno
Jessica Shoup
Stephen Stocker
Miles Wentzien
McKayla Woodall

*Cover designed and illustrated by Lakin Abbey, Jayme Bigger, William Bihn, Tanner Hocker and Kaytlyn Roberts

Dedications

We would like to dedicate this book to all the ghost story lovers, thrill and chill seekers, who have motivated us to write our best; to the children of the United States who like to write books; to our Richardson Elementary teachers, teacher associates and friends who have taught us to treat others fairly and who have helped us revise our stories; to our families for supporting us and giving us great ideas; to Mr. Carlson who inspired us to get started and gave us all an amazing chance to succeed in publishing a book that people will like.

About the Authors

This book was written by 45 students from two fifth grade classes at Richardson Elementary School in Fort Madison, Iowa. Richardson is a relatively small school in comparison to other districts, with 457 students and approximately 70 staff members. Many families deal with a low socioeconomic status. Fort Madison, with a population of approximately 11,300 people, is a rural community located along the banks of the Mississippi River in Southeast Iowa.

Students, ages 10 – 11, vary greatly in ability and learning styles. They were surprised at how much work went into writing a book!   At the beginning of the process, they worked with partners to come up with an idea for a ghost story. Using trait-based writing, students drafted a plan, then wrote multiple drafts, revising and editing with each update. Throughout the process they received guidance from their teachers, teacher associates, and received advice from peers and family members. Students gained experience with team work as they cooperated with partners to come up with a final draft. The entire process took three months, from October 2007 to January 2008.

Both classrooms promote positive thinking and actions that align with mission statements, which were written by students at the beginning of the school year. Character and relationship building are also reinforced in weekly class meetings, where the classes identify themselves as "The Boeding Family," and "The Starlight Express." Students from both classes look forward to writing again, and many have plans to publish their own book!

Table of Contents

Preface

Just "Wait"

Okay, right now you are probably wondering what the big deal is about reading this story... I know you are extremely excited and ready to read all of the creative ghost stories in this book. Trust me, you will enjoy them! However, if you read this you will understand not only how this book came to be, but how important waiting is...

Have you ever heard your parents, friends or teachers say, "Good things come to those who wait." I used to think they just said it so I would stop complaining. (Have those thoughts ever crossed your mind?) I never really believed the words, until it happened to me!

My husband, Eric, and I planned a relaxing Sunday Brunch at Alpha's restaurant. We arranged for his parents to watch our energetic children: Nadia: 4, Isabella: 2 and Leif: 9 months. We figured the longest we would wait to be seated was 15 minutes. This was the normal wait in Fort Madison, Iowa. We calculated our wait and brunch would take about one hour. (That seems reasonable, doesn't it? We thought so and we went ahead with our plans.)

When we entered Alpha's there were more people waiting than we had anticipated, but we just figured we'd have a slightly longer wait. So we didn't think much of it, and put in our name. The lady said we should be seated in 20 minutes or less. (I bet you have waited that long and it didn't bother you.) We just waited... and waited... and waited... More people began coming in to wait. Before we knew it 20 minutes had passed and only half of the people there before us had been seated. We had seen people leave, so we assumed others would be seated shortly. Ten more minutes passed, and there was only one more small group before it was our turn.

Finally, it was our turn to be seated and I was excited as I was getting a little hungry. The food smelled so delicious that I began to taste it. Then they called a group that arrived after us. At first I was mad. I almost said something, then I noticed there were four people in their group, so I thought maybe they were waiting for a specific table for the two for us. Five minutes later, a group of two was called. Now I was getting really annoyed because it had been 40 minutes. This was all taking much longer than I wanted. We were supposed to be half way done eating by now and we weren't even seated! I went up to ask the waitress how long she thought it would be.

I kindly told the waitress my name, and she looked at her list. She said she did not have our name down. I couldn't believe it! Our name wasn't even written on the list. I looked at her oddly and with a little frustration. She looked again at her list and said, "Oh... I know what happened; I must have written you down as a different name... I think I wrote down 'Jones' instead of Boeding... No wonder no one answered... Okay, I'll put you on the list, now you will be next. It should only be a few minutes..." My mind was raging uncontrollably and I was deep in thought, "What!? They didn't write our name down? How did they get Jones out of Boeding? I bet they wrote too fast and couldn't read their own writing!" (I'm sure none of you have ever done that.) With a bit of annoyance I said, "Okay." After all, we'd been waiting this long, what was a few more minutes? So I went back to wait...

As I waited, I noticed an older gentleman, pacing. His hair was a frosted silvery white and he was wearing comfortable jeans and a loose fitting white jacket. He had been waiting almost as long as we had. By now the small waiting area was flooded with customers who were really tired of standing around. The restaurant was obviously very busy and waitresses were hard to find. The phone was ringing, but no one answered... Then it rang again, and I observed the oddest event.

The older gentleman answered the phone, "Good Morning, Alpha's... I don't know. I don't work here. I'm just waiting to eat. I'll let you know when someone comes..." He laid the phone on the stand and looked around to flag down a waitress... I couldn't believe it! Did a customer just answer the phone? I had never seen that before. I had to laugh to myself. I couldn't blame him as the phone was annoying to listen to. Besides, he was only being helpful because he didn't have anything else to do, but wait. Ten more minutes passed, making our total waiting time about 50 minutes. Boy, was I hungry, but we knew we were next. We might as well wait a few more minutes.

The waitress called for a group of six. I was completely flabbergasted... I was speechless. I was so upset I didn't know what to say. It was like I was frozen in time, but everyone else was moving around me. What was going on?! No one even answered. Then something caught me by surprise...

The older gentleman, who had answered the phone, excitedly responded, "We have six! Us, those two and those two," as he pointed to us and another couple. I was taken back. Was he serious? I had never been volunteered to sit at a table with complete strangers before so I didn't know how to respond. Should we sit with them? We didn't even know them? I was supposed to be having a relaxing brunch with just my husband and I... I was very disappointed that my plans seemed to be spoiled. (I bet you can remember a time when things didn't go quite like you planned.) Anyway, my husband convinced me that it would be fine, so we followed the other two couples to a table of six.

We all sat down and introduced ourselves. Eric and I were seated next to the older gentleman and his wife, which was the best decision we ever made. Right from the start, the older gentleman was talkative and full of spirit. It didn't take long for us to find some connections. He was a customer at the bank where my husband is Senior Vice President. His place of employment was only a few blocks from the bank. His wife was a retired teacher... The list could go on and on, but I will get to my point. I found out he was an author, printer and publisher! At our brunch, we set up a date and time he would come to share his career with my 5th grade students and one thing led to another... So, as the saying goes, "The rest is history..."

Here we are now at the end of my story and I want to leave you with this important life-long lesson. As I waited for a good meal, I ended up with quite a bit more than I bargained for; I ended up with interesting conversation, a new friend, and a field of opportunities for my fifth grade students. As you waited to hear the end of my story, I hope you realized that "good things really do come to those who wait." Wait no longer and read these intriguing stories from Richardson Elementary's 2007-2008 5th Grade class.

Wendy Sudarshini Su Boeding
5th Grade Teacher

Chapter 1

Alamo

By Alexa Bell-Randolph and Courtney Ford

Have you ever herd of the Alamo? Well I have I've even been their. There was a huge war between  the people from Mexico and Texas. The war started because the Mexicans took the freedom from Texas. The people from Texas weren't too happy. So they decided to have a war for freedom. The war was long and frightening. Nobody knew that a magical cat and dog were walking through the walls. Watching the dreadful fight until it was over.

Before the war started an evil witch named Sidney put a curse on the war. So the war will never end, because Sidney loved to do bad things I mean really bad thangs. Sidney would do stuff nobody even dreamed of doing.

The cat and dog knew about the curse. The cat and dog ended up as ghosts too, because they were still in the walls when Sidney did the spell. They had no idea that Sidney was doing the curse at that specific Time. The cats name is Honey and the dogs name is Wendy. Wendy wanted to end the curse. Honey never

wanted the curse to end, because she was an evil cat. So they both left the Alamo and went their sprit ways. It took them both a long time before they reached a resting point. Wendy was going to a good witch and Honey went to a really evil witch.

So after a few days of traveling, Wendy finally got to a good witches house. The person Wendy was going to her name is Alexa. When Alexa herd barking at her door she opened it to find a dog looking tired, like he ran fifty miles even though she really didn't she ran more. Alexa decided to let the dog in. The dog kept barking like he had something to say important. Wendy decided to make a potion to let the dog talk. She needed a frog's leg, a vampire's fang, dog's fur. It took her a few days.

Meanwhile honey was meowing for a long time, before the evil witch Courtney even bothered to listen. She finally opened the door. Honey kipped making noises Courtney could make out what honey was trying to say to her. So Courtney decided to make a poition. Just like Alexa did. She needed a frog's leg, a vampire's fang and a piece of cat's fur. First Alexa and Courtney went to the dentist office in another realm of magic like creatures, for a vampire's fang. The realm of magical creatures is where magical people and animals live. It was just

their luck because; two vampires were on the schedule to get a

tooth pulled at the same time. After that they needed a frog's leg.

So they went to a store. They asked for a frog's leg. It only cost

a dollar, so now they just need one piece on dog's fur. One piece

of cat's fur. They for some reason got that at the store to. They

went home and mixed the potion.

They had to drink the potion. Wendy drank the potion

and started talking. She had so much to say she didn't know

how to say it. So she started out talking about the curse. Wendy

said, "They fit every full moon the ghost would fight again.

Then Wendy told her that an evil with named Courtney her

great great grandmother snindey was the one who put the curse

on the Alimo. That way only Courtney could end the curs. By

poring a secret potion on the roof of the Alamo saying a spell that goes like this. But they knew Courtney probably wouldn't do it.

Courtney let honey drink the pot in. Honey started out by saying. Along long time ago you great, great, great, grandmother sandy put a spell on the Alamo. So the people who fought would still fight as ghosts. The only way the curse will end is if you pour a secret potion on the Alamo and recite a spell that goes like this, remove this curse my assister made and demolish it from harms way. There is a good witch named Alexa that wants you to end a curse.

Alexa wanted to meet Courtney at Courtney's house. So she went their and knocked on the door. Courtney opened the door with a big sigh, like someone died. She knew it was the witch because Honey told her. So as soon as Alexa asked Courtney she said no. Alexa begged and begged like an hour later she said yes, because Courtney felt the need to do something good. So they went into the pantry in the kitchen and found the ingreadents. So they both made it. Alexa and Wendy had the spell in her hand.

Then they couldn't wait to do the spell. But they can only odd it on a full moon. So they waited till next week to come as the days past they grew sick of waiting. Finally it was the day of a full moon. So that nigh the got all they needed a went to the Alamo. They new the could only do it at night. So as son as the town cloc rang twelve times. They it was time. They waited a few seconds because the clock was so loud, like a train was going by. So the dumped the potion on it and recite the spell. The wind blew lights flickered an a few minutes later every thing was well. The curse finally was over but over all you should never take others FREEDOM!

Chapter 2

Death Zoo

By Savannah Lorton and Angel Richardson

Do you have a zoo in your town? It's Halloween night in St. Louis, Missouri and the wind is blowing hard. The zoo is closed because two people died there. There are ghosts in the zoo. The ghosts died by barbwire as sharp as shark teeth, and by rusty nails by a lion, in a cage. These teenagers heard about the ghosts at Halls Ice Cream where they work. The teenager's names are Eric, Jaslene, Kevin, and Natasha. There personalities are, Eric is a helpful person, Jaslene is a friendly problem solver, Kevin is the joker of the group, and Natasha, well she's also a friendly problem solver. They decided to go because they wanted to know if it was true. They decided to go on October 31st. Today is October 31st.

Their on they're way to the zoo. They get to the zoo and the doors are locked. So Kevin breaks the glass and unlocked the door, they go in, they hear noises. They are in the main section, where the computer, check in, and where the important stuff is, like keys. Kevin, and Natasha go upstairs, and on they're way up, they hear creaks in the stairs. They go to look for things out of order, like broken glasses. The ghosts want them to GET OUT!

Eric, and Jaslene went down to the basement. They hear trees hitting the window. Natasha, and Kevin found broken eye glasses upstairs. Jaslene, and Eric found a farmer glove. It's a light brown farmer glove. In the basement they heard wind whistling. Then Jaslene calls Natasha on her cell phone and tells her to meet in the main section. Now, they're in the main section.

They tell each other what they found. So, they go upstairs and look threw the microscope, to see if they could find any finger prints on them. When they looked threw the microscope they saw fingerprints on the eye glasses and the farmer glove. So they left them there, they all went to the basement. They all went to a different room in the basement to look for things out of order.

Then they met up in the middle of the basement, and told each other that they didn't find anything. So they went upstairs to look for different things, but they didn't find anything either. They went to the main section and went to the microscope. Then they looked at the fingerprints again, next they start hearing their names being called. After that they started seeing faces in the windows, and they saw long, dark shadows. They heard talking, they found out, it was ghosts because they said they were ghosts.

They heard, three, hard, knocks on the door. The ghosts names are Larry, and Gregory. They knew this becuz it was in the newspaper. After that they went back to the main section, and they

25

heard loud sharp scratches on the wall. They said that they were scared.

Kevin said "Lets keep looking,"

"Eric said madly "fine," But, he said if we hear or see anything else to go to the main section. Next they split up, and they switched spots Eric, and Jaslene go upstairs, while Natasha, and Kevin go down to the basement. The ghosts kept following them. Then they heard a scream from the main section

Natasha screeched "What was that ?"

Natasha calls Jaslene to ask her if they can leave and Jaslene told her to meet in the Main section. So Eric, Jaslene, and Natasha, and Kevin go to the main section and they agree that their going home .

Kevin yells "NO, the adventure has just began," but they leave anyway .They all leave except Kevin.

Kevin's like "I don't care I don't need you, "Kevin goes upstairs and finds a door. He thinks it's a secret door.He open's the door and the alarm goes off, ERT, ERT, ERT, ERT. He runs to the main section and trips over a nail and dies, because he fell on his head.

The cops come and found him dead. He had his funeral and his old friends, Natasha, Jaslene ,and Eric go to it. Hes funeral was so sad they left early. A year later there's four more teenager's go in, and the same thing happens to them at the same time. Kevin and the ghosts became friends becaz there ghosts. That's why you NEVER go in places that are closed. ECSPEALLY ZOOS!

Chapter 3

Ghost Girl...Ghost Girl...Ghost Girl

Written by: Lakin Abbey and Kristen Meierotto

Tanner is really jumpy when he hears noises. He goes out because he hears a noise down by the dock. He sees a beautiful girl and she has long blond hair. She looks like she's from a long time ago but she has pretty clothes. He goes to her and then she disappears.

He goes to tell his mom, Jenny, what he saw but she doesn't believe him so he goes and gets her and brings her down to the dock to show her the beautiful girl. When they see her, they ask her what her name is. She says her name is Jaclyn and she tells them that they moved into her house. It was her house when she was a little girl. Jaclyn fell in love with a man named Jordan, a week before Valentines Day. On Valentines Day he proposed to her on the dock, but her foot slipped in. Jordan ran to call 9-1-1, but she was already dead. The ambulance came and she was already skin and bones because there was something in the water that ate all her skin off. They buried her in the cemetery.

Jordan was lying on her grave, crying, and couldn't stop. That night he left for Disney World. He saw Walt Disney and told him what happened to his girlfriend. Walt gave Jordan a nice room.

Jordan was running down a hallway and saw Jaclyn. He tried to talk to her, but she couldn't understand him because she was a ghost. He got really scared and went to his room and said Jaclyn was really freaky!

Jaclyn went down to the lobby. She started to talk to some people. They got really scared so they ran to their room as fast as they could. Then she came through the walls and everyone was so scared that they all left.

While at Disney World, Jordan meets a new girl and her name is Jenny (Tanner's mom). He asked Jenny out and she said yes. She went home to show Tanner her new boyfriend. Tanner started to roll his eyes and frowned. Jordan, Jenny's boyfriend, looked at him funny. After that, Tanner's mom said that Jordan was going to live with them. Tanner went to his room stomping off.

She said, "Why don't you go talk to him, Jordan?"

He said, "OK, I will go talk to him."

She said, "Thank you."

Jordan said, "It is ok and, he is like my son now."
Then Jenny made a funny face at Jordan. The next day
they woke up and he was making breakfast for them
which made Jenny so happy.

Next week after that Jordan asked Jenny to
marry him on Easter. Jenny started to cry and Tanner
got really mad at his mom because she said yes.

The next day they were planning their wedding.
They were going to get married in two weeks and Jenny
was so excited! Tanner was really mad and he really hated
his mom's boyfriend. Jenny went to go get her wedding

dress, while Jordan and Tanner went to go get a tuxedo.

Then Tanner and Jordan went out for lunch and Tanner liked him a little bit more. After that day

Tanner asked Jordan if they could go see "Happily Ever After." When the movie was over, Jordan asked Jenny if their wedding could be the next thing to think about it.

Next week came along and their wedding was happening. Tanner was the ring boy, and his best friend, Lexy, was the flower girl. They went on their honeymoon, to Las Vegas. After that day nobody was able to see the ghost of Jaclyn.

Chapter 4

The Ghost in 302

By Lexy Bergthold

& Jessica Shoup

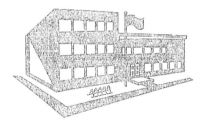

In the year of 1976, on a full moon, the upstairs halls were dark, and the fog outside was thick. Fred L.A. Johnson was only 10 years old when he died. It was the first day of school when he was coming down the red stairs that were pretty high. His squeaky, old tore up shoes were untied. He tripped and fell, but the halls were silent, except for the sound of Fred's shrill screaming and terrified crying.

28 years later, a boy named Roy, which was wearing a white T shirt and blue jeans, was in dentition once again for putting thumb tacks on his teachers' chair, because he is a trouble maker from problems at home, because his parents got in a fight and then were divorced. When dentition was over it was 5:00PM after school, so he went up stairs to get the homework of the wild life book report, he forgot. He walked in and the door creaked closed behind him. Then the teachers' radio atomically turned on by it's self to the oldies she made them listen to at reading. Weird things started happening in the room, like the blinds went up and down. He tried to open the door but it wouldn't budge, he couldn't get out! He was stuck in the creepy old classroom.

Kelsey, his sister, started looking for Roy but she couldn't find him. Before she tried opening the door to the classroom the handle was shaking she didn't know what was going on, but it wouldn't open from the outside. She asked Bill the, janitor, for the keys to open the door to the classroom. She tapped his shoulder he yelled' GET OUT OF HERE"! She thought the ghost was inside bill. She ran as fast as she could to find her mom.

Roy was very scared he was locked in an old classroom. When the lights flickered on and off finally it attracted Fred so he came out of the vent. Papers where flying everywhere! Roy hid under the group of desks. Roy found out that bill has seen the ghost before when Bill got Roy out of the classroom. Bill saw the ghost fly out of the room and go to the kitchen down stairs. Bill, Roy, and Kelsey went into the messy kitchen. Black pots and pans started flying every where. When Roy got there he found his mom "Sara who was there to pick him up, she was terrified and Roy was relived.

The water in the sink was running, but all sudden the janitor, bill, came in and started waving a mop everywhere in the air, the ghosts is scared of mops because when he was

walking he tripped over a mop and they spilled all over him. Then the ghost flew back in the vent and we never saw him except when he comes to visit for revenge.

That's why you should NEVER! Forget your homework. And Roy learned that he should NEVER put thumb tacks on his teachers' chair.

Chapter 5

Ghostly Princess

Written by: Ceairra Barker, Hanna Goebel, and Kaytlyn Roberts

One beautiful moonlit night in 2oo2 Mindy and Eric, a happy engaged couple of twenty-three, strolled hand in hand down a well known beach on Mackinaw Island, Michigan. With them was Mindy's tiny white poodle, Pebbles, who was happily sleeping in her purse. Mindy was wearing a silky sky blue top along with a flowing knee length white skirt. Her hair was blond, flowing in soft beautiful ringlets to her lower back. Along with that she carried a purse that matched her top, in which Pebbles sat. Eric was wearing a white tank-top and camouflage pants. Mindy strolled along beside him in the moonlight, lost deep in thought about the thick book she had just read that afternoon.

The book was called <u>Ghosts of Mackinaw Island</u>. She thought about the girl in the story...

The girl's name was Elizabeth; she was the princess of England and had decided to come to a party in America. It was a cool summer night, August 6, 1887, when Princess Elizabeth rode up to the beach in her beautiful carriage drawn by her horse, Pepper Anne. As she rode up, everyone turned, stared, and bowed. She was wearing a beautiful gold silk ball gown and beautiful white ball flats with gold bows. She also wore elbow length white gloves with gold trimming. Her hair was as beautiful as her clothes, the color of midnight flowing smoothly down to her lower back. After many hours of dancing she grew tired and went in to check her make-up. While she was indoors some how a fire started, and the mansion burnt to the ground. Princess Elizabeth did not make it out in time. Some say, her ghost now haunts the place where the mansion was and is searching for her arch enemy who started the fire that had killed her.

What Mindy and Eric didn't know was that Eric's great-great-great grandfather was Princess Elizabeth's arch enemy and was the one who burnt down the mansion to kill her. He had wanted to kill her because he had also killed her father so that he could become the King of England. Eric also looked exactly like his Great-Great-Great Grandfather.

Mindy came back to her senses as Eric called her name. "Mindy did you hear something?" Eric asked suspiciously.

"No," Mindy answered. "Why?"

"Oh never mind." Eric said. All of a sudden a deep growl came out of Mindy's purse. Mindy slipped her hand into her purse and felt Pebble's nervous ear twitching. Mindy felt her heart beginning to race as she twirled her hair on her finger. Eric noticed this and put a protective arm around her shoulders. It's nothing really he said to her. "Pebbles is just going psycho."

"He is **NOT** going psycho!" she answered. All of a sudden they heard an eerie noise behind them. Princess Elizabeth's ghost came out of the trees by the beach. Mindy let out an ear piercing scream and jumped behind Eric.

Eric stared at the ghostly figure floating towards them. He began to walk back slowly making Mindy stumble behind him. He turned around and was about to begin running until he saw Mindy laying pale in the sand, she had fainted. She lay motionless on the ground; her face was as white as the sand she had fallen on.

Big dark clouds rolled over Eric's head and a huge explosion of thunder started a down pour. A strike of lightning came down and lit up the whole scene. He saw Mindy slowly rising out of the corner of his eye. Out of the corner of his other eye, he saw the ghost of Princess Elizabeth floating eerily towards him. He heard Mindy scream and felt her grab his arm. He grabbed her hand and began to run. But then he heard a frightened bark and Mindy screamed" Pebbles!" Eric tried to grab her before she ran away but she slipped out of his grasp and ran towards the ghost and Pebbles. Right before the ghost reached Mindy she snatched up her purse, Eric grabbed her free hand, and they ran as fast as they could down the sandy beach. Eric felt a clammy hand on his shoulder and something sharp, but he pulled away just in time. They ran until they thought they could run no more. Eric stopped and pulled out Mindy's cell phone, quickly he called her private jet and in the time of two minutes it landed. Two men jumped out of the jet and stood stunned for a moment seeing Mindy's appearance.

Then Eric shouted "Don't just stand there! Can't you see there is some thing wrong?" The men grabbed towels and wrapped them around Mindy. When they got to Mindy's house she took a bath. She was so terrified that she didn't speak for one whole entire day. The next day Eric had reminded her about the wedding they had planned.

"Oh, when did this get decided?" asked Mindy. Eric answered, "A few months ago". Mindy finally remembered that tomorrow was the wedding June, 7 2002. That day had gone by fast! Everything turned out perfectly, just as they had planned.

After the wedding they were thinking about the ghost that put its clammy hand on

Eric. So they went and found information on Princess Elizabeth. They found out that the man who had killed her was Eric's great-great-great- grandfather. From then on Mindy and Eric thought it was a scary, frightening feeling. Every once in a while they gave a little laugh about that night. Through the years they never saw the ghost again.

Chapter 6

Halloween Night at the Arch!!!

By Abbigale Gordy and Shelby Kemper

It all started in dentition, at James Madison middle school, October, 31ˢᵗ, 2000, on a dark scary Halloween night. It had seemed the moon was shining more then ever as if there was a light bulb inside.

Fred and Robert are both 14 year olds, from James Madison middle school. Fred and Robert were sitting in dentition doing homework on little desks that had old dried up boogies sticking to the bottom of the desk. They could feel and hear them crunching every time they'd move. When Robert realizes he forgot his math book upstairs in room 301. When he came back to the dentition room there was a piece of homemade Halloween candy on his desk there was a note attached to it in the note it said: Happy Halloween Robert!! Best wishes to you!!! You're Friend Fred. He gobbled down that candy like a dog swallowing a dog biscuit.

They were walking home when Robert said in a nervous voice "I didn't feel very well" and fainted. {This was planned by Fred with poison candy .nobody knew why. It could have been jealousy or it could have been something going on at home.}Then Fred bent down to see if there was a pulse but could not find one. He stood up and made an evil smile and ran away before someone would see.

Later that night when Roberts little sister Lizzie was trick or treating with her friends Abbey and Anna. She tripped over Robert and started to cry because she realizes that it's her brother Robert. She ran to her mother, Elisabeth as fast as her little legs could run. To tell her to come see and her mother hugged Lizzie and began to sob. Then her mother said "its time to go home." "Who would do such a thing"?

Then Robert came back as a ghost and realized that Fred gave him poison candy on purpose. Robert was really mad!!! He was so mad he could hurt somebody so he did. Can you guess who he hurt?!!!!!! Fred!!!!!!! He hurt Fred so bad he died. Nobody will forget that night of 2000. <<<! Fast Forward! >>>

It all started in dentition on October 31st 2007 a dark scary Halloween night. There are three boys one of the boys name is Gavin. Gavin is 14. He is sweet and innocent .This is the first time he'd ever been in dentition or even a fight. He was trying to stick up for his friend Jacob and came out with two black eyes. He lives with his mom. He is an only child as far as he knows. His moms name is Stephanie, Steph for short. She spoiles him because she feels bad about her and her x- husband getting divorced when Gavin was two his dad moved to Texas and got married. Gavin was really sad. The next boys name is Jacob he is 14 also. He is best friends with Gavin. Jacob is quiet .He has 1 younger sister named Lexi, she is very curios and likes to be a follower . Last but not least is Nick. He is 14 too. He is always getting in to trouble. His favorite thing to do is play sports and getting dirty and is really hyper because he has ADHD. He doesn't realize this yet but Robert the ghost is his brother is trying to keep them safe by telling them to hide and things like that because the world is dangerous.

Back in dentition Jacob forgets his math binder and reading book. He goes upstairs to get his stuff. When he got upstairs he went to his classroom, 301. Once he got upstairs he

49

tripped on a meter stick .Then he looked up the widows were open, and in the closet the jackets were floating in mid-air. He jumped to get his but he couldn't reach. So he went to his desk to get his stuff. When the boys came in the room and every thing shut and a big gust of wind went though the ceiling fan and it turned off. The boys went to go leave but the door was locked All of a sudden wind pushed them against the wall. Then something began to write on the board, it said!!! GET OUT!!! YOU DON'T BELONG HERE!! then the door slammed open and they ran out of the classroom and ran in to Jacob's little sister.

"What were you guys doing in there?" Lexi said in a questioned voice.

"We don't know but something is going on in the school!!!" said the boys.

"I have to go to the bathroom" said Lexi. "Us too" said Jacob. When they came out of the bathroom, Lexi was gone!!!! All of the sudden they saw BIG shadows and heard whispers but couldn't make out what they were saying. Then they heard Lexi scream! They started to run they got to the dentition room to see Lexi. "Did you see and hear that?" said Lexi "yeah that was pretty creepy wasn't it?!" said Nick   "I want to go home" said Gavin as Jacob said "That was weird"

"Hey! Did you know the arch is haunted on Halloween?"

Said Nick "really" said Lexi "don't believe that stupid nonsense, yeah right" gasped Jacob.

"Are you serious?" Gavin asked

"If its nonsense then you wouldn't be afraid to stay there TONIGT! Now would you?" said Nick

"No!" said Jacob as he whispered maybe to Gavin

"you   wouldn't last 10minutes there!"Warned Jacob

"would to" said Nick

"if your not scared will both go tonight so will you Gavin?"

They both said at the same time yes

"cool can I come?" asked   Lexi

"sure" said Gavin as the other two yelled No!!!! at the exact same time.

"There's no way your going with us to the arch tonight. You will get to scared and want to go home" said Jacob

"Fine" said Lexi.

Jacob, Nick, and Gavin went to there houses to ask there parents and get there stuff they needed. Their moms all said yes. They were walking to the arch when they heard a few cars but the rest was silent as soon as they got there they put up there tents and sleeping

bags to go to bed. Then they realized Lexi had been there the whole time. She brought her

sleeping bag but no tent. "Hey" didn't we tell you couldn't come? "Yes but mom said I

could!" "So" the point is we told you to stay home! "Fine you can stay but sleep outside there's

no room in here!" "Ok" said Lexi. All of a sudden she heard an owl howl so she got scared and

asked Jacob to sleep in there he said Fine but we'll have to move the cooler out side so Jacob

and Nick got up to move the cooler and Lexi moved into the tent. By the time the boy got done

the other two were sleeping already.

Later on in that night around 2:00 AM Lexi woke up and got scared and went home.

Jacob had to go to the bathroom so Nick and Jacob went down two blocks to Jacobs house to

go to there bathroom when they got back to the tent. Gavin was Gone! They went to go look for

him. When they go to the Arch doors they were unlocked so they decided to go inside to look

for him they went up the elevator it went really slow up and stopped right at the top room

they got out and went in the room all of a sudden the elevator went down really fast. They

stayed up until it came up again when it came up there was green glow, and what had looked

like dark red blood foot prints they got on and it looked like the foot prints had moved in the

room. The elevator went down really fast.

That was really scary" said Jacob "Yeah!" said Nick in a scared voice. When they got

back downstairs they went on the tent and Gavin was sitting there eating cookies and candy.

Then Jacob said "Where were you this whole time?" I want home to get a snack the boys Just

laughed and went back to sleep.

The next morning was a cool, crisp, foggy, and breezy morning. They picked up

there stuff and walked home. The red foot print was really Frank and Robert but they weren't

trying to hurt anybody they were trying to teach a lesson about betting on stupid stuff. The

green light was a firefly though. So as you know the arch is NOT haunted on Halloween night

or any other night. It may be scary though. Hey Jacob, Nick, Lexi, and Gavin. Want to go to

the Arch with us tonight, said Nick`s little brother. "Yeah, it'll be fun," said Gavin's little

brother. "Come on please!" said Jacob's little brother. Not again said Jacob, Nick and Gavin and

began to laugh so will you said Nick's little brother!!! No!! Said the three boys. Nick never

found out that Robert was his brother but he will soon.

HAPPY HALLOWEEN!!!!!!!

Chapter 7

The Haunted Mansion

Written by: Lexi Gonzales and Rhyan Amrine

Two years from tomorrow, the ghosts of a young couple who just had married haunts a house. The couple had only been  married and living in the house for one month. They thought they had found the perfect house, but the night before Halloween someone walked in their front door. The couple came downstairs and they didn't see anything.

Just then, they saw a dark shadow. The husband went in the kitchen to get water and walked out of the kitchen, set the water down and sat down. They saw the black shadow moving towards the water it poured poison in the water without them knowing. So they drank the water, collapsed and died. Every year, they haunt that same house on the day before Halloween.

My name is Mark. I have two friends named Addie and Elizabeth. They don't know it yet, but we are going to explore the house of the young couple who died on the day before Halloween. Elizabeth will be so freaked out but Addie won't. Addie is really brave, but Elizabeth will bring at least two mirrors, because when she is nervous she pulls out a mirror.

In one hour Addie and Elizabeth will come over to my house and I will give them the news! Addie and

Elizabeth just rode up on their bikes and walked in the door.

"I'm going to the haunted house do you want to come?" I asked

"Ok but how are we going to get there without our parents knowing?" Addie questioned.

"Um, we will tell our parents we are going to a Halloween party," I said.

"Tomorrow will be perfect because it's the day before Halloween and that is when the house is haunted."

Today Addie, Elizabeth, and I are all going to the house to explore. We have ten minutes to get ready and meet each other at the park. I was the last one to get to the park. Now we are ready to go to the house.

We arrived at the house at exactly seven thirty. We have exactly three and a half hours to explore the house. When we opened the door we felt a big burst of cold air. We saw a huge chandelier that had a dim light. Past the parlor we saw a staircase that circled up a long  way so we all went up to the very top and Addie heard glass breaking and Elizabeth saw a radio plug in by itself and heard music so she pulled out her mirror! Addie and Elizabeth told me what they heard and saw. So we all went down stairs to the dining room and we saw a broken glass vase lying on the floor.

"That's the glass I heard breaking!" Addie exclaimed.

"That can't be Addie!" I said.

"I heard it!" Addie said. "Yeah Mark,

I saw a radio plug in and play," Elizabeth

whispered. Just then we saw two glasses of water

moving toward us.

"OK guys I believe you now!" Then we saw two

black shadows moving into the kitchen. We all

screamed even Addie! We ran into the parlor! When

we got there we saw lots of pictures of the young couple

and even my parents! "Wow, my parents must have

been good friends with them!" We saw a piece of paper

and a pencil and saw the pencil write something. Then

the note blew in my face. I read the note

aloud. It read:

"Why aren't your parents here?"

We ran into an old grand piano as

we ran away from the note. We heard music and

Elizabeth said, "That's the kind of music your parents listen to Mark!" Then I ran into a big bookshelf with pictures of them at their funeral in their parlor.

"Everything is moving into places where we try to run!" I screamed

"I know" Addie whimpered.

Hey Addie are you getting scared?" Mark asked

"No, I'm just thinking." Addie said.

Just then we saw the two black shadows again.

"Um. . . Mark you're walking pigeon-toed again, you must be thinking too hard!"

"Come on guys," Mark whispered. "Let's get out into the kitchen!"

"No because I saw a butcher knife in there!" whined Elizabeth.

"Oh come on Elizabeth you're such a baby!" Addie teased. "It's not like someone is going to pick it up."

"Yeah but there are ghosts in there!" whimpered Elizabeth.

"So, I hope you brought more than one mirror, because when your mirror sees your face and hears your scream it's going to break!" argued Addie.

"That's mean, Addie" whined Elizabeth

"Stop fighting guys it's annoying!" I yelled

"Yeah Elizabeth" Agreed Addie

"I'm talking to you too Addie!" I said

"Let's just go into the kitchen and look around.

We all went into the kitchen and saw a chalkboard that said Menu. We saw a piece of chalk write on the board again.

Why aren't your parents here Mark?

Then the butcher knife that Elizabeth saw picks up and flew through an open window and then everything went dead silent.

"I think we should go now because its ten o'clock and our "party" ends in a half an hour. On the way out they didn't hear anything. After Addie, Elizabeth, and I left the couple's house it wasn't haunted at all. Someone is living there now, because there are no ghosts or scary things after our visit.

Chapter 8

The Haunted Statue

By William Bihn, Tyler Landrum, and David Nagel.

George Washington, and the person who made the Statue of Liberty. Fredric Bartholdi Are ghosts because George and Fredric are both dead. George Washington wanted to see the Statue of Liberty. He thought it was cool because it was big and there was enough room. So he wanted to live there. Fredric Bartholdi Thought it was his finest piece of work. They knew that 9-11 would happen.

Together they keep it safe and clean so 9-11 won't be the statue.

They didn't want 9-11 happening to the Statue of Liberty.

It was a foggy Halloween night. Oct. 1986, a cold

Friday. Three teenagers named, Tanner, William, and Jim meet

at the Statue of Liberty .They were looking in the museum

looking at some nic -nacs when the doors closed. They heard a

very loud scream upstairs. They started to run upstairs. When

they got there, they were the only ones there.

They heard a loud BANG downstairs. They go downstairs and see a black cat. It had big green eyes and big claws. The cat attacks William he gets four deep cuts. Jim said it was a stray cat and they attack at random. The cat suddenly disappears in mid air.

George Washington appears in front of them with an axe. he said" get out Tanner replied" We would if we could"!

Suddenly there was a cold draft that went trough the room. William asks "what's the axe for"? George yelled" GET OUT!!!!!!!!!!!!!!!!

After that he disappeared. "How did he disappear" asked Tanner. "Maybe it is a ghost". "Don't be kidding there is no such thing as ghosts" told William. Suddenly the lights went out. It was pitch black. Jim said "I can't see you guys". They hear heavy footsteps. The lights come on and George Washington and Fredric Bartholdi are in front of them with rocks in their hands. They wanted to throw them at the kids to try to hurt them so they could capture them. But they kept missing Tanner and Jim but they hit William once by George.

They were so scared they ran so hard into the door it came unlocked. Jim said "it's unlocked". They ran into their blue boat at the dock and hid in there. William peeks around the and sees George running out. They get out of the boat and run to the other side of the statue where he couldn't see them. William peeks around the corner and he is standing right there. They went back to the boat. They run back to the boat and the rock flew right by Williams head. It was so close to hitting him he could hear it whistle by him. They all jump into the boat where he couldn't see them. Tanner picks up the key and tries to start it. It wouldn't start. Tanner said "it's not going." He sticks the key into it again it turns on. They were about half way back to the city when they heard another boat behind them. They had to drive the boat around in till Fredric gave up. They were far away where he couldn't see them. He shuts the boat off and about five minutes later he tries to start it and it doesn't start. He looks at the gas and it is on the E. Tanner said said "OH - NO!" They hear the boat coming so they all jump out. They have to swim back. Fredric comes up to their boat and looks in it. Nobody is in it. So he drives it back to the island and tells George about it.

The kids get back into the city about thirty minutes later. They learned never to go back to the Statue of Liberty on Halloween night, or any night. They also learned not to mess with a national treasure. Because , It might just be haunted.

Chapter 9

!!!Homerun!!!

By Bryson Abbey and Parth Bhoja

This is about Derek Lee a real Cubs Player. (And he's not really dead.) We chose him because he's one of our friends favorite baseball players.

The game was tied the score was 7-7. The Cubs were against the Rangers. It was a really big game. Derek Lee was up to bat and he had a horrible strike out, which caused the Cubs to lose the game 8-7. This caused the coach to be the

laughingstock of the really big game.

One week later it was a dark and foggy night. It was so dark

that you can't see your hands in front of you . The moon was out

but it wasn't too bright. Derek Lee

was walking to the Cubs

playoffs. He didn't look both

ways before crossing the street and BAM!, A yellow semi as

big as a huge boat hit him really hard. The driver was laughing an

evil laugh so loud the whole neighborhood could hear him as he

saw the dead body of Derek Lee, and the driver was his coach!

It was the night Derek Lee passed away the moon was

still out the team was really sad and scared about losing an awesome player. All of a sudden the Cubs started losing 0-7 in a game rematch against the Rangers, because Derek Lee was scaring the players at every base, by trying to hit them in the head with a bat, because he was really mad at the coach.

After the game which the Cubs lost Sam and Bob went to the Cubs Stadium to play catch, that's when they saw the ugly, pale ghost of Derek Lee hitting ghost baseballs with a ghost bat. Sam and Bob knew they had to trap the ghost, before the World Series [which is in 10 days] or the Cubs will lose the biggest game of their life. Derek Lee wants to get revenge on the coach for running him over and doing the same thing to the coach.

So Sam and Bob put the coach in a box of concrete

filled with water as bait for the ghost. Then take him out before

the ghost got the coach. Just before he got the coach they

pulled him out. Sam and Bob closed the door and locked it with

a lock made of stone and Derek Lee returned to his normal

body but he was still dead. Everything went back to normal and

the Cubs won the World Series.

When Sam and Bob were walking home from the World

Series late around 12:00 midnight that's when they heard a

creaking noise louder than a cars horn they knew Derek Lee

turned into his ghost body and escaped. They knew he wanted

to get dark revenge on the coach. When they ran to find the

ghost they saw him in the coach's house. The ghost got into the house by going through the wall. He took the coach by his shirt, got some rope, tied him up and threw him on the road.

Then the ghost got a big, huge semi. Just as the ghost was about to run the coach over Sam and Bob grabbed the coach off the road. The semi missed and crashed into a building, and the semi blew up. Then the ghost came out. Sam and Bob hit the ghost with a ghost bat from a ghost hunting store [which can actually hurt a ghost].

They pushed him in the concrete box filled with water because it drowns them. This time they locked it with a ghost lock, [which can keep a ghost in a box]. Everything turned back to normal and this time Derek Lee stayed in the box forever and can't escape because he has no feeling thanks to the ghost lock.

The lesson is to look both ways before crossing the street.

Chapter 10

Horse Back

By Brian Hayes and Christopher Andries

"Get off my big green perfect yard, you darn kids!" yelled Mr. Bell. Mr. Bell is always grumpy. People think it's because he is short. Fat and has to work with horses. He lives in the middle of nowhere. But everyone was wrong it were because his wife died. His wife was very nice but she was just too old, she was 73 years old. It was not Mr. Bells fault, but he still blamed himself. She died at the diner table; she went face first right into her spaghetti DEAD. Mr. Bell still has the big bulky red chair she always sat in, and watches her favorite TV show. Some times he would sit in it and remember her cooking and the smell of her perfume she war some times.

One night he was sitting in the red chair and fell a sleep. When he was asleep he had a dream that an unfamiliar face was floating across the room from him. The thing was standing right in front of them. He stuttered "W-ho a-re you."

"I'm the ghost of Mr. Carlson leave this house." said the ghost. This is where I was going to live, but I died before I set a foot in the door." Boomed, the ghost of Mr. Carlson.

"H-o-w d-I-d y-o-u die?" Asked Mr. Bell.

"Want to know how I died?" Well I was trying to take my horses to the stable and I hit the tree branch." said the ghost in a smaller voice then usual.

Mr. Bell was trying to get out of the dream but now he wanted to stay and listen.

"I was on my oldest horse Lightning and all of my other horses followed me to this house where I died," said the ghost of Mr. Carlson.

"I still don't know how you died," said Mr. Bell.

"Huh, I just told you how I died turn on your hearing aides!" Yelled Mr. Carlson's ghost

"But you hit a branch why'll riding your horse, can't you just get up? I can understand laying down a little while, but dieing is the part I don't get." said Mr. Bell. Mr. Carlson stood there a while before he *answer*.

"I hit the branch and got trampled!!!!!!!!!!!!!!!!!"

Yelled Mr. Carlson, as loud as he could be.

"Ok, ok, ok, you didn't have to yell." said Mr. Bell "Just leave this house ……. Now….. Please" said Mr. Carlson rubbing his forehead.

"You won't let me leave." hissed Mr. Bell. Mr. Carlson snapped his fingers and Mr. Bell woke up. "When" Mr. Bell woke up from his dream he heard his horses neighing. He looked at all of the horses they where all running around Crazy. Mr. Bell went to come them down he realized two of his smallest Horses where missing he looked about half an hour but he could not find them. "Mr. Bell" was tired and hurt from looking so much. Mr. Bell Couldn't sleep *that night. He finely fell a sleep* at 1:10 the next day. Mr. Bell went to feed the horses and noticed two more horses where gone. He looked around and found some horse tracks. He went and followed the tracks. He ran into a creepy tree and got chills down his back. He walked around the tree and noticed that the tracks stopped. At the tree Mr. Bell stopped wondering and went to the store.

And about a video camera 35 minutes later he went back to his house with his camera to see if he could find the person who was stilling his horses. He put it in front of his horse stables door turned it on and went to take a nap. He woke up looked out the window had noticed both doors where open. He walked over to the camera and saw it was turned off. When he got in the house. Now he knew it was not an animal, unlace it was a monkey but, but why *would a monkey*, Mr. Bell couldn't believe he just thought of that, monkeys in Boise, that's a crazy thought, were would it live, why would it need horse. "Well there are a lot of kids." Thought Mr. Bell. He thought for a little while, and declared to get another camera and hide it some were, so he could catch the man who was stilling his horses.

Mr. Bell came back with another video camera. He thought it would be a good idea to but it in the big window of house his house. Mr. Bell went to go make a T-bone stake with a sailed with beans and an ice tea with a lemon. Mr. Bell went out to his living room to watch TV and eat his dinner. He looked out side and forgot to feed his horses so he went and feed them. After that he walked inside and looked out the window.

And saw a foot go into the hole of the tree. He

went outside to look in the hole of the tree. When he

look inside a squirrel attacked him. When he was

trying to get it off and he was running around and

went to the horse stable and all of his horses were

gone.

Mr. Bell ran inside and called his mom and

asked if he could come and stay with her for a while.

She said it yes, but it was it's freezing in this house,

bring me some firewood first. So he took his ax and

went to the creepy old tree where he saw the foot go

in it and cut it down.

A few days later Mr. Bell went driving by his

old house to go to the store and he saw all his

horses were back and the tree was back too. He

realized that the ghost was real and it was mean

because it wanted him to get out of his house. He

was kind of nice because he brought his horses back.

So now you know never look back while riding

horses because you could get seriously injured or

die.

Chapter 11

House of Bad Memory

Written by: Miles Wentzien and Austen Brand

In 1999 we were leaving Shottenkirk with our
brand new car. Before we knew it, we were at the
ancient haunted house named House of
Bad Memory! It was said that real
ghosts were attracted to it so we
brought our cameras in.

The real ghosts were attracted to the screams of
the people visiting the haunted house. These screams
are what made the ghosts come alive. The ghosts have
been here for so long, in the same place, that more than

eight of the haunted house guides know where the ghosts will be. But most of the guides look too scary that people are freaked out and won't ask them where the ghosts are. Every night the population of the ghosts increases because of all of the screaming.

We were waiting in line for 2 hours, hearing screams and seeing kids run to their cars. An hour later, a lady had a heart attack. After that nothing happened, so we begged our mom to go back home, but she said, "No!"

We were up next and it was extremely dark so mom went to the store first and bought us two flashlights and a bag of snacks. We walked into the dark and scary house. The first thing the old man with red eyes, pale white skin, and a long white beard said was, "Look at that chair and take a picture of it ." So I did. I was sure that nothing was there but sure enough there was a red and orange orb. So I continued and heard a loud screeching scream and said, "Did you hear that?!"

But they said, "Did we hear what?"

"That scream."

"No!"

"It must have been an orb."

"It was," my mom exclaimed.

I asked, "How do you know?"

She said, "I got a picture of it." So we went down to the basement.

The guide pointed at the couch and said, "Go feel the air". So mom went over and touched the air around the couch. As I was eating my snack , what was eyeballs she touched the air and screamed. I through the eyes up in the air and they stuck to the ceiling I grabbed my camera and took a shot their was a pale blue ghost. She said it was 100 degrees cooler. Five minutes later their was a party behind us we grouped up with them and watched a movie but I got scared half way there so we left early I was scared silly.

When we got home the lights were out and the TV was off so I tried to turn it on but it didn't work. So for the first time in three months I went to bed with out a TV. I was freaked out! Then the TV came on I looked up frantically but saw nothing there! At that point I was holding on to my brown teddy bear. Then I heard popcorn popping, which was impossible because we don't have a microwave or popcorn. I decided to sprint into my moms room. I made it and tried to wake her up but as soon as I touched her I felt a strong shock. At that point I was extremely scared! I thought I was going to have a heart attack. I grabbed my coat, looked at the TV, and stopped. I saw the lady who had the heart attack, just hours earlier, jumping out of a plane. I was scared so much I had to get out of there. As I was getting ready to leave the TV shut off. I turned around and saw a green mob coming after me. I screamed and ran out the door in a panic!

As I'm running outside at midnight I hear a rumble in the distance. I feel a screeching pain in my back. I see green eye sized balls coming at me. I dove to the ground, turned around and saw that only one hit me. The rest of them made a scary face on the willow tree behind me.

All of the sudden I saw the ghost come off the tree and start coming toward me. I started sprinting towards the house when the house popped off the ground and grew ten feet.

I turned around and ran to the street. Then the face caught me and I fainted. The ghost thought I was dead and left me alone. I woke up in the morning on the side of the road. I walked inside thinking it was just a nightmare. I went into my moms room to make sure she was there, but she wasn't. A strike of lightning hit the bed. I started running to the phone to call the police but the line was cut off. Then I realized that my mom had to go to work. I was home alone and started running to moms work.

As I was running, every car on the highway started following me, honking. There were no drivers in the cars! I walked into my moms work and heard voices but saw nothing. I frantically picked up the phone and tried to call my mom. I got a hold of mom and asked where she was. She said she was sitting in bed. All of the sudden I got tapped on the shoulder and heard mom saying its time to go to the Haunted House called

The House Of Bad Memory!

Chapter 12

LIFE OR DEATH

Written by: Steven Hinojosa and Frank Davis

DANGERS DO NOT READ!!!!!!

It was a crisp autumn morning. We were on a trip to

Camp Running Leaf. We were waiting for my

Grandpa with his Van. We started to get

in the car. We could almost smell

that camp air. We were here at last. We started to get

out of the car when we saw our counselor he took us to

our cabin. We put our stuff on our bunks . Later that evening we started to get ready for bed.

We went to breakfast. There were eggs with blue yolks. We were hungry but didn't eat. Just then the counselor came in we hid our eggs. He yelled at a kid named Nicky. He had hid his eggs in his shirt. Now every body was done. Then the counselor said you have to do the hurdle and the mountain climb. First we did the hurdle. We got in line to the hurdle. We started running then we realized there were chainsaw blades. We ran to the mountain climb. We were getting ready to climb. But before the counselor said "we are looking for a skeleton bone". We started to climbing up Skeleton Mountain. We found skeleton cave. We grabbed two skeleton ribs. We started to run toward camp. When we got to camp. After we had dinner we went to bed. In the morning we had break feast and went to our cabin. Then we went on a canoe ride of (doom). We made it to the other side and back until the counselor through us out of our boat!

Something skimmed my leg. Then I said there it goes again. Then "Frank" said "no your joking". We were petrified. At dusk we finally got out. The counselors were so ugly. We went into gruesome details. They had maggots coming out of their eyes and

then we realized their teeth started to crack.

Then we heard a weak voice out of the darkness. It was our counselor. Run for it I said. We were running to the door until they blocked the door. We will never get out Frank said. Suddenly I saw an air vent. We started to climb but they hissed come back! I don't think so I said. We ran to the lake to swim away. They started to swim until we saw the lake monster! It started

to eat the counselors. Then it started to

feed on the kids. We ran up the sidewalk until we came

up the car.

I said let's go. We went to the parking lot grandpa was

there we got in the van an both said let's get out of

here. Grandpa went fast .when we got home grandma

said lucky you get to go to camp again. We both said

not again!

Note to reader!

My name is Frank. I like sports of all kinds and food of all kinds, such as

Pizza, Spaghetti, Steak. Here's my very favorite sport: Baseball. But that's

enough about me here is my friend Steven. Hi my name is Steven. I like to play

Dodge ball, Soccer ball and Kickball. My favorite foods are Bread sticks and

Spaghetti. My favorite movie is "Sky high." We're not very old were only 10 years

old.

Chapter 13

Overcoming Rides

By Jon Geoffrion

I wrote this story because I don't believe in
ghosts. I thought it would be fun to know how to
overcome your fear. Not all rides are real.

Have you ever overcome your fear? Well Brian had
to. He was thinking that he might throw up during any
ride. Brian is twelve years old and is a guy who wears a

hat with a green shirt and bright blue pants. He is funny because he jokes around like a clown. His friend Christopher was eleven and had blue shirt with baggy pants. Calm like a cat. Jonathan was 13 is cool and has Nike shoes, dark blue black pants and red shirt.

One day Brian, Chris and Jon went to Worlds of Fun. Brian was nervous of the rides, especially the Bomb because it was noisy.

Chris said, "Don't be scared there just rides."

Jon was impressed of all the rides because they're very big and very high. Jon told Brian that his friend Tyler told him that once one of the rides got stuck because the power went out. He felt nervous because they go very high in the air.

"Wow, look at the size of these rides. They are big like sky scrapers!" exclaimed Jon.

Chris said, "Come on."

Brian, Chris and Jon went to a ride called The Topper that spins around like a top. Brian felt good about the first ride because it just spins a little. Then they went to a water ride that you ride in canoe. It felt cool for Brian to kind of taste what a real rainforest feels like. After that they went to teen rides, because the rides are high. One was called The Diver you were in a submarine and then you dive. Brian felt better as he learned about the ocean life.

After that they went to Oceans of Fun, which it's next to Worlds of Fun. Brian felt relieved when he went to Oceans of Fun because not many rides go high. Oceans of Fun is a water park that has a lot of water rides. The

 famous one is Mega Monsoon. The ride starts out your in a boat and you go up a steep escalator and then you turn and drop down. You go so fast that a huge wave splashes the people on the bridge. Then they went to Mushroom Village were water comes out of these big mushrooms. Brian was having fun going under the water.

Chris said "Why don't we go to different rides on our own and meet at McDonalds, at 12:00."

"Great plan" said Jon.

Brian went to rides for kiddies like the Snoopy plane and Charlie's train. He did this because he wanted to exercise before he went to the big ones. He was sort of nervous about the big rides. Jon went to water rides like the Log Race, Jungle River, and Mega Monsoon because it was hot outside. Chris went to rides that went high like the Bungee Jump and the Sky Dive. Soon it was 12:00 they all met at McDonalds. Brian orders a Big Mac with fries and a Large Coke. Chris got two Double Cheese Burgers with fries and medium Mr. Pib. Jon was so hungry that he got two Big Macs, large Coke, and a large fry. After that they all had caramel sundaes.

"That was tasty!" said Jon.

"After this we go to the Dragon King." said Chris.

They were glad to eat so they can get energy because they don't get scared on other rides.

Then they went to a ride you are in a car and bombs are exploding everywhere. Brian felt better after the ride was done, because sounds of the bombs hurt his ears. The last ride they went on was the Dragon King, because it was bigger than the rest of the rides. They got on the train and the ride started while they were going they heard deep rumble all of the sudden a dragon came out.

"It's a dragon" some one yelled in the audience.

The dragon roared and disappeared beneath the ground.

Then they saw a nest full of eggs.

"It's the dragon king's nest" said Brian

in a whisper. He felt scared.

Then a there was a crack, and

another one. Soon a dragon head popped out of the egg.

The train started again. Soon the dragon appeared with

her babies it roared, it blew fake fire on the train and

disappear. Soon the ride was done and they were outside again. "Well that was fun I think. That ride is cool." said Brian

"Well like I tell you if you have a fear overcome it." said Jon

"Plus the power didn't go out." said Brian. Brian felt better when he overcomes his fear of rides. He thanked his friends because they helped him out. Then they went home. Now, Brian thinks he can go back by himself and maybe try the big rides first, because they are the best.

Chapter 14

Plane Crash At Alcatraz

By: Jayme Bigger and Jessica Fitzgerald

When Nick aborted flight 14 he didn't know the plane was going to crash .The plane was white with a red 14 on the side. Flight 14 was leaving Alabama and landing in California. Nick is a tour guide touring in California. He is short with dark brown hair with blonde highlights. He was dressed in a really nice black suit. He is 21 years old. Nick is going to take a tour at Alcatraz, because he is interested in historic landmarks. Alcatraz is a Prison, on a small island, just small enough to fit the prison and a small shed in the back. People thought it would be hard for convicts to escape because it was on an island.

Nick got onto the plane. When he was seated he went through his bag looking for the brochure to Alcatraz. While he was looking he found an old newspaper that's headline read "Man was arrested for gas station robbery"

As Nick was fumbling through his bag a lady was panicking and demanding to be let off the plane. Nick wasn't paying a lot of attention to the lady so he only heard something about being afraid of heights.

Nick just got comfortable when the pilot announced that something was wrong with the motor and the plane was going to crash. As soon as the pilot finished speaking, Nick heard a loud boom and the plane started falling to the ground. Nick blacked out for a couple of minutes because something hit his head. When he became conscious he found out that he was the only survivor of the crash of flight 14 and he felt sick because of the gasses and fumes from the plane crashing. The plane landed on a small island not to far from a bigger island with a building. Nick dove in the water and kept swimming towards the building. After five minutes, Nick reached the building. He saw a sign that reads "Welcome to Alcatraz Prison. Tours are available."

Nick went inside the prison to see if anybody would be able to help him or to tell the police that the plane had crashed. Nick looked everywhere. Every floor, all the cells, everywhere he thought people would be. He kept walking. He kept looking for people. He got to a door. The door had a small plaque that reads "Joe the Janitor."

Nick stood for a few minutes, in front of the door. Reading the plaque over and over again. He opened the door and he saw a tall, gray haired man wearing a uniform. The man turned around.

"Hi, my name is Joe. I'm the janitor." The man said politely.

"I need help! The plane crashed! I'm the only one left! You've got to help me! Please help me!" Nick said quickly.

"Slow down. So the plane crashed. You're the only survivor you need help. Are you hurt?" Joe asked.

"No, but....I'm so confused about this whole thing. Wait, where is everyone? Why are you the only one here?" Nick asked confused.

"The prison guard took all of the convicts to another prison. I'm here because the manager wants me to clean up all the cells before I go to the other prison" The janitor replied.

"Where did the plane crash?"

"On a small part of land about a five minutes swim away from he-" Nick was unable to finish his sentence because Joe opened the door and walked out of the closet.

"Where are you going?" Nick asks.

"You'll see." Joe answered.

Joe lead Nick to the back of the prison. He went into a shed. The shed looked old and gave Nick chills because it looked haunted. The shed looked like it had never been used. It had green vines growing around it. Joe came out dragging a motor boat.

"Nick, help me carry this boat to the water" Joe commanded.

"Sure. Wait, I don't remember telling you my name." Nick said a little scared.

"*How would I know your name if you didn't tell me?*" Joe asked.

"I'm not sure but-" Nick's voice was drowned out by the roaring of the motor on the end of the boat.

"Are you going to get in?" Joe asks, yelling.

Nick gets into the boat. He didn't say a word the whole ride. He was lost in thought about the plane crashing and how to get help. When they got to the part of the island where the plane had crashed, Joe got out of the boat and started checking the plane for problems. Nick was still trying to figure out what was happening in his head, so he didn't leave the boat. Joe looked at the motor. He muttered to himself about mixing gasses of some sort. He looks at Nick and gets back into the boat.

"Someone mixed gasses. The oil is where the gas should go and the gas is where the oil should go. Either someone did that on purpose or they picked up the wrong jug when they put the gas in." Joe yelled so Nick could hear him over the roaring of the motor. Nick just nodded.

When they got back to Alcatraz, Joe dragged the boat to land, tied the boat up, and went inside. Nick followed Joe to the janitor's closet.

"Stay right here. I'm going to go call for help." Joe instructed. Nick waited just like Joe had said to.

After ten minutes had gone by, Nick got tired of waiting so went to explore the prison. He went to look at how unique the cells and the weapons were. They were nothing like the other cells and weapons he had ever seen before. Nick would love to give tours at Alcatraz. Nick heard a whisper behind him. He looked back and saw a shadow. He was a little frightened. Mice scattered across the floor. The shadow moved in front of him.

"I'm Mary. I'm a ghost I've lived hear at Alcatraz for ten years." said the shadow. The shadow came into focus. It was a beautiful platinum blonde girl with her hair tangled into knots.

She was dressed in a tattered white dress. She wasn't very tall, but wasn't very short either.

"I'm Nick. Ok....well....how did you become a ghost?" Nick asked curiously.

"Well, about ten years ago it was my wedding day and my fiancé had to work. In fact he worked here at Alcatraz. But any way, I searched just about everywhere for him. I was on the last floor and I was walking up and down the halls. I saw one of the convicts stick his hands out of the cell. My fiancé was turning the corner. The convict took the keys away from him. I was too frightened to say anything because the convict had the keys. The convict unlocked the cell door. I didn't notice that the convict had a weapon until he used it on my fiancé. I was turning around so I could get away. I was crying so he might of heard me. He caught me. He kept me hostage. He left me there. No food, no water. I ended up dying of starvation." Mary tells her story. When she finished, she was really sad.

"Hey, Nick! Why didn't you stay where I told you to?" Joe asked angrily.

"I was tired of sitting around so I came to explore the prison." Nick replied.

Joe didn't say anything so Nick kept walking. He thought about whether Joe could see Mary or not. Nick was turned away from Joe and so was Mary so they couldn't see Joe pull out a knife. Joe put his hand on Nick's shoulder. Nick turned around and Nick gasped as he fell to the ground.

Joe walked away yelling "Don't trust strangers! Some of them may be convicts in disguise! Besides, that's what you get for putting me in jail! When I robbed that gas station I didn't think any employees would call the police, but you did. I was put in prison for ten years. Don't you remember?"

Mary gasped looking at Nick. She was crying.

"Get help, please!" Nick said to Mary. Mary ran as fast as she could. Past all the cells, down the stairs, and out the front door. The stairs creaked as she went down them.

Mary heard the roaring sound of a motor boat once she got outside. Mary looked out and saw a boat with about ten people coming towards Alcatraz. As they got closer Mary worried about Nick. The boat stopped and all the passengers got out.

Mary yelled "You've got to help! Nick was wounded by a convict in disguised as a janitor! He's wounded really badly and- and, he needs help!" Mary's words ran together because she was so scared that Nick wasn't going to live. Mary talked to them not thinking about if they saw her or not.

"What?" said a tall man with red hair. Before Mary answered, she thought that they must think she's still alive.

"Follow me" Mary said leading the man and anyone else that wanted to follow up the stairs towards Nick.

Nick waited patiently in pain. Joe was packing his clothes, weapons, food, and water from the closet. While Nick kept bleeding. He thought about if Joe was really Joe. If what he said about the plane was true, if he was meant to be the only survivor, and if everything was planned. Mary burst into the room where Nick was laying.

"Here he is!" she yelled while sitting down next to him on the floor.

"Yes, I need a paramedic as fast as you can at Alcatraz prison. We'll wait outside. A guy was wounded" said the man, talking on his cell phone. The man put his phone in his pocket and picked Nick up.

"I need someone to help me carry him outside. Oh, and by the way, I'm Kevin" He said.

A brown haired woman helped Nick. Once they got outside they had to wait about ten minutes for a paramedic to show up.

Nick was carried on a boat to land. Where they could put him in their vehicle and take him to the nearest hospital. Mary was crying really hard. The police came shortly after the ambulance vehicle had left. They wanted to know how Nick got hurt and who did it. Mary told the story and she gave the description of the prison convict, Joe.

It was about an hour later and the people at Alcatraz got news that the police had caught the convict. But nothing about Nick. Mary was afraid that Nick was too injured to live. Mary was crying, even when she was laughing. Mary was laughing because Kevin told her jokes to cheer her up. The thought of seeing the horrible sight of what happened to Nick, made her shiver. When they finally got a call from the hospital, Mary was already worn out from crying so much. But when she heard that Nick didn't live she cried hard enough to make someone think that she hasn't cried in a long time. After Nick's funeral, Mary was in the hall of Alcatraz, wandering around. She saw a dark shadow. When the shadow came into focus Mary saw Nick. Nick felt good getting to see Mary again. He wanted to visit Mary.

"I've learned my lesson not to trust strangers." Nick said. Nick and Mary thought that they would live happily, until they got news that Joe (the convict) had escaped from jail.

*<u>Note to reader</u>: When we first wrote this story our title was "Flight 14 Down." It is a coincidence how our story ended up at chapter 14. Maybe it was the work of a ghost...

Chapter 15

Randy Wayne and the Train

Written by: McKayla Woodall and Adrian Gomez

One morning, Randy Wayne Woodall, redneck deer hunting, history channel watching, chicken eating fool was drinking his coffee at the table. After his coffee was gone, he got ready for work. He puts his work clothes on. Well anyway he gets into his silver Chevy, and goes to work, but he gets caught by the train. So he is late to work. But Lily Merette was waving at him when he got inside. It's just another hard working day. After work he drives home during rush hour and as soon as he got home the phone rang. A good friend of his said, "Lily died just about 10 minutes ago."

"How did she die?" he asked.

"By a train," the worker cried.

"The train, but how?" Randy asked.

The worker sobbed, "She tried to race the train but the train won and Lily lost."

That night Randy could not fall a sleep. He was watching the news on TV; it showed the news caster by his job. He was wondering why she was in front of his job? The news caster came on and said, "There was terrible a accident this evening with RMSF coal train. Lily Merette died this afternoon by a train here in Fort Madison. The train was going about 30 miles an hour when Lily raced the train, but the train won. This is KAQH news!"

This made Randy sadder than the RAMS losing to the DALLAS COWBOYS! The next day he went to work and seen the ghost and said hi! And every one looked at him! That day there was a bad thunder storm. It went on for five days and it stared to rain more! It started to flood on the railroad tracks and the factory. The lights went off and they thought they felt cool air going through their bodies. And they knew that Lily was behind this! They heard a voice talking to Randy! Lily said, "I'm OK, I got hit by a train and I'm OK."

Randy whispered in a shaky voice, "I miss you, are you going to come back to work with me?

Randy was even sadder than before when she said, "I'm dead, Randy. I can't come back and she turned the lights back on and then someone made her madder by yelling at her!

"Why did you shut off the light you creepy ghost?" All of a sudden, a table gets slammed on the window and it shattered!

Then someone's sweet voice saying, "Please stop!"

Then someone said, "We aren't listening".

Then we heard a demanding like voice giving them a demand, "Be nice or I'll wreck the place!"

Then everyone said, "We'll be nice! we swear!"

Then the voice came back to a nice voice and said, "Thank you," and the lights came on and the next morning everyone was scared to come to work.

Then Randy was working on a machine and felt a tap on his shoulder and looked. All he saw was a fast black flash and when Lily died that's what color dress she was wearing, but when Lily died that's all

he could ever think about. It was tragic but it's a good thing because she would come every now and then. So Randy wouldn't miss her that much.

* Note to reader: This story is part real. Randy Wayne Woodall is Mckayla Woodall's grandfather. He is 52 and his best friend

died about a year ago. We just took the story from Gleason's and rewrote it for you and she didn't die of a train, it was a fatal stroke.

This book is in memory of her and in the story we changed her name for people who know her. And the reason why she died of the train is because Adrian loves trains. Plus when there's a story afoot, team work is best and every idea counts!

Chapter 16

Riverview Park

Written by: Tanner Hocker & Stephen Stocker

It was just another day in fifth grade. Stephen as usual was making something out of erasers, staples, and pen ink. Tanner was in his seat starting on his planner and Accelerated Math like he was supposed to. Stephen was the average kid at 12 years old. He was as smart as most kids when he wanted to be. Tanner was 11 years old and was really smart most of the time. Those two boys were really good friends. After school the two boys would often hang out at Riverview Park, like they were tonight.

 After school Stephen and Tanner went to Riverview Park. As the tale says, there is supposed to be a young Indian ghost down at Riverview Park. The two boys don't know about that though. Nothings ever happened to them. Stephen and Tanner regularly play on the playground for a while, then they go down to the river bank to skip rocks and listen to them skid across the water. Before they go home they sit down on the river bank and talk usually about hunting and sports.

The ghost of the Indian came from the Fox tribe. He was a young Indian about the age of 25 years old, but nobody really knew. The Indian had long black hair that shimmered in the light, but was covered by a headdress. He was an Indian that traded with white people from the Old Fort (in Ft. Madison Iowa.) The Indian died in a great battle at the Old Fort. These battles often happened, which sometimes lead to a lot of deaths.

Stephen and Tanner went to Riverview park after school. They did what they usually did, such as played on the playground. Then when they were skipping rocks they heard the sound of rocks grinding together. It was creepy and loud! Stephen and Tanner froze and looked at each other. The boys looked at the water and, saw sitting on the river bank what appeared to be a young Indian ghost. He was glowing in a light *blue, gray dim light*. Stephen and Tanner looked at each other and asked if they saw the ghost. They both said "yes" to each other.

The Indian looked at them and started walking toward them. Stephen and Tanner looked at each other. Tanner said to start running! The two boys took one more look at the ghost, and took off running and ran and ran until they got to Stephens house. Since then no one   has ever heard the ghost, seen the ghost, no ones ever mentioned the ghost again. From that day on the boys go to different places such as the skate park, and the basketball court after school instead of Riverview Park.

Chapter 17

ROBERT

By Kelsey Heidbreder and Nicole Crespo

This story is about a horrifying ghost, he scares little kids that say his name. It started in Fort Madison Iowa. Sandra is a most popular girl that lives in Fort Madison, Iowa. Sandra's whole school thinks she is beautiful. She is a victim of the ghost. Why is she a victim you ask? [Read on and see]

Important news bulletin, little ghost boy is haunting little kids that say his name. They say he wants to haunt kids his own age. This little boys name is Robert, so do not, I repeat, do not say his name! He recently died in a bad car accident. He was sitting in the front seat of the car without a seatbelt on and a semi came and hit him and his mom. They both died but when the semi hit his mom yelled Robert really loud so now Robert hates people to say his name. Do not say this boy's name he is very scary, Robert is terrified of tom cats and German shepherd dogs, nobody knows why, so get one very soon! Robert is a pale, short little boy, and looks five or six years old.

Sandra watched all of that on television. Though she did not believe in ghosts, she told her mom about the show she watched on TV about Robert.

"Mom" Sandra hollered "I just saw on TV, a ghost boy named Robert haunts any kid that says his name."

"There is no such thing as ghosts" Sandra's mom carefully replied."

"I know." Sandra squeaked as she left the room.

That night Sandra wakes up to a very horrible sound. Robert hid in the corner of Sandra's small closet. He said stop saying my name. Sandra yelled for her mom. Her mom came running up the stairs. Her mom asked "what's the matter."

Sandra exclaimed "I saw a ghost."

Her mom said "there is no such thing." Again that night, Sandra wakes up and finds Robert under her bed. She screams for her mom. Her mom came very sleepy. Her mom said there is no such thing as ghost and went back to bed. Sandra woke up again that night with Robert right in her face and this time he GOT HER!

The next day nobody could find Sandra. Nobody except Robert knows.

The next part of this story talks about a small, shy boy named Ted that goes crazy for seeing Robert. Ted, is a shy short red haired boy, that does not know about Robert. Ted calls his best friend Robert that lives in Orlando, Florida. Of course Ted asks for Robert. I think you know what happens that night. That terrible night Robert haunts Ted.

Ted is in his living room watching "Ghost Hunt", when he falls gently asleep. He wakes up at 1:17 exactly in the morning and sees Robert's face. He calls for his dad. His dad comes down with a broken baseball bat. Ted's dad says to sleep in his room.

Ted can't sleep. Just days later Ted ends up in a mental hospital because Robert scared him so much by him just seeing Roberts face, that's how scary he is.

This is when the other Robert gets haunted.

The little boy Robert that lives in Orlando, Florida is Ted's best friend. They got separated last summer when Robert moved away from Burlington, Iowa. Ted gave Robert the nickname Rob. Rob has no clue about what happened to Ted. Rob tries to call Ted's house. Ted's mom answers and nicely asks who was on the phone. Rob tells Ted's mom who it was, then asks to speak to Ted. Ted's mom tells Robert what happened to Ted. Rob was really sad that night, so he could not sleep.

Robert haunts Rob that night because he heard Rob say his name over the phone.

When Rob is trying to sleep that rainy night the door gently squeaks open so only Rob could hear it. Rob was very scared and quickly asked who was opening the door. It reveled, a small, pale ghost. Rob loudly asked who he was. Robert says who he is. Rob says to the ghost "come sit and talk with me". Robert tells Rob he will listen for ten minuets. "Why have you come to haunt me" asks Rob. I do not like when people say my name. "Why" asks Rob. Robert tells Rob about the car accident and how the Semi hit him and about his mom saying his name. The ghost says he will bring back everybody he haunted if he could visit Rob every week; because he does not want to scare the friends he had when he was alive. Rob agrees to this deal, and Robert brings back everybody that was missing. From that day on Robert never haunted again. And kids this is why you always listen to the news.

Chapter 18

Scratched Out

Written by: Meagan Hoening, Megan Derr, and Hannah Puls

The Cash family took a Christmas vacation to Orlando Florida.

Then they went to their hotel and dropped of their luggage. After

that they went to Coco Beach. Mom was tanning, and Dad was

playing football with Johnny. Then they went to Ihop and Johnny

saw the ghost of Hermit his black cat. Johnny told his mom and

dad when he came back from the bathroom. He said he saw

Hermit. He was very scarred. They didn't believe him, so mom

checked his head for a fever. Then they went back to the hotel and

Johnny's parents tucked him in. He fell asleep and later he woke

up screaming an ear piercing scream.

When he was finished screaming he started drawing pictures of his cat, his pictures were some what scary. After that his cat showed up on his bed then his parents opened the bedroom door and Johnny said, "Kitty!" His parents looked on the bed.

They got dressed and went to the Roadrunners Drive Through. They had Fried Bunny Ears, Roadrunner Bagel, Frog Eggs, cheese, and a Skunk Milkshake. After that they went to Sea World. Johnny saw his cat surfing on a whale his cat looked like an ant on the Shammou Whale. Then they went to the gift shop to buy Johnny whale sunglasses.

They went to MGM Studios and got on a lighted ferris wheel. Then they got off and all of a sudden Johnny saw Hermit juggling  on the ferris wheel. Then the kitty ride fell off and nearly killed them. After that they found out how it fell off and it was because one of the Road Runner spinning cup hit it and broke it. They went back to the hotel because Johnny wasn't feeling well.

That night Johnny didn't bother eating. So Johnny just fell asleep and dreamed that his parents had a car accident and died. So then he woke up and started drawing again. All of a sudden Hermit showed up and confessed he killed his parents.

What had happened at the car accident was Hermit locked them in the car and pushed them off the cliff into the freezing waving ocean. The waves were so high that it took the car down in one wave. That night they froze to death. Before he pushed the parents off the cliff he left a scratch on the window.

20 years after Johnny became a famous singer and sold million albums. His C-D was called Johnny Cash. Ever since he had his cat Hermit got bigger and bigger so he called his next C-D was called

Cat and Cash. Now they are best pals and Johnny still draws

pictures, but only about his cat and his C-D's.

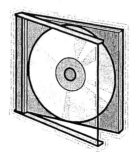

Chapter 19

"Shadows Don't Scare Me No More"

BY Dakota Salerno, Dajada Meredith and Shawn Carrell

I saw the shadow on the wall. Dad turned the light off

only five minutes before. Every

night that shadow appears after

my dad leaves the room.

I lay in my bed with the cover up to my chin. "Please stay away," I said. When I turned over in bed, it would move or get bigger. I would get so scared. How can I get rid of this shadow?

I finally was able to shut my eyes. It felt like I slept for many hours, but it was only 15 minutes. When I opened my eyes, there was the shadow looking at me. I screamed, "Stay away, stay away."

My parents came running in and turned on the light. "Are you alright?" my mom asked.

My dad asked, "What is wrong? You were screaming."

I told dad about the shadow in my room. He asked, "Where was the shadow at now?"

I couldn't find it. Dad told me to go back to sleep. I asked my mom to stay with me till I went to sleep. She sat beside me and I felt safe. I finally fell asleep.

Why is this happening to me? A person is suppose to get rest in their bedroom. All I ever get is scared.

Each morning when I get up, I am so tired. I don't get any sleep because the shadow is always there. Someday I hope to be able to go to bed and sleep through the night.

It is almost 5:00 in the morning. Mom comes to wake me at 7:00. Another day of falling to sleep at school. I don't get my work done. Then I get into trouble with my teacher.

When I got home, my parents were waiting for me. My dad wanted to know why I can't sleep when I go to bed. I tried to explain to my parents about the shadow in my room. My dad told me to just get over it. My mom told

me she would put a nightlight in my room.

We had a quiet supper. My mom is a very good cook. I had to do my homework. It is 8:00

p.m. – the dreaded time in the evening when fear comes knocking at my mind's door.

My mom told me it was time for my shower and brush my teeth for bed. I tried to sneak into my bedroom. My mom was there with the night light. She plugged it into the wall. I turned the lamp off, but there it was. It didn't work. I pulled the covers up over my head. When will it go away? My mom came in to check on me. She saw the curtains were open, so she closed them. Mom told me that the street light was too bright and it would keep me awake. When she left the room, I sank down into my bed. My eyes were closed so tight they hurt.

I thought I would see if the shadow was still in my room. I opened my eyes and it was gone. I wanted to jump up and down!!! Instead, I snuggled into my bed and went to sleep. It was the best sleep I have had in a long time.

The next morning before I got out of bed, I looked around the room. There on my dresser was my baseball trophy.  It was then that I realized that the shadow of the trophy was what had been scaring me all along. I got dressed and went to breakfast. I had a great day at school that day................and looked forward to 8:00

....and a good night of sleep.

Chapter 20

TIME

By Shylynn Hart and Gillian Cates

Today was the day of the huge tragedy of the Twin towers.

Shylynn and Gillian were learning TONS and TONS about 9-11

at school. After school they walked and talked about 9-11 as they

returned to there home on 3105 pine court. Suddenly the girls

looked up to see a mysterious girl who was

running away from someone or something clomping her feet very

loudly. The girls were wondering why

she was running so very fast so they

followed her to a building that was

open 35 years ago and now shut

down.

Once they got to the building they opened the door and

saw New York, and then realized that they time traveled all the way from Maine to New York. Shylynn shut the door so very lightly so no one  could hear. The girls looked up to see an airplane crash into the

North Tower.

They were so frightened that Gillian jumped back and hit Shylynn in the head. Shylynn fell to the ground and let out a horrible scream.

"Shylynn get up! We have no less then 20 minutes to find that girl", said Gillian.

Shylynn jumped up and said, "There's that girl." The girls rushed toward her. The mysterious girl handed Gillian the note. The address said 3102 Cherry Pike Street.

Gillian read it aloud. *Dear Anna Lee, 9-11-02 is the day I had past. I was in the South Tower. It was five minutes after the North Tower went down. I was trapped in the elevator at the time and, right when I got to the top, BANG! I died.. Sorry I didn't give you this sooner I died quicker then I thought*

Your beloved mother

May Pan

Shylynn said, "Let's go inside the house so we can get transported back to present time but still in New York," Gillian agreed. Just as soon as the girls stepped inside the house sure enough they got transported back to present time but still in New York. The girls walked to the house. Someone who was probably in their thirty's opened the door.

"Hello. I am Anna Lee. Who are you?"

"You're Anna Lee?" the girls chimed together. Then the girls fainted. Anna Lee carried them in the house and woke them.

143

The girls handed her the note. Anna Lee was in shock while she was reading.

"Well I didn't know she died in the twin towers. I...I... I... thought she, uh, died in a car accident," stuttered Anna Lee.

"NO," yelled the girls.

"Well I'm glad you gave this to me", said Anna Lee.

"OH NO," said Shylynn. "MOM And DAD , they will ground us for life."

"Lets go," said Gillian. The girls left with out saying goodbye they found the building that transported them to the past and went in the girls got there just in time to get punished for telling their parents that they were time traveling but their parents thought they were lying of course so they learned their lesson. Anyway about that mysterious girl. Some say that she is a ghost and that she visits New York every 9-11. Some say she's not a ghost and doesn't come back at all. The girls haven't seen her since then but will always remember her. Do you believe that she is a ghost?

Wait don't put this book down yet, that is not all that happened. The girls started dreaming of 9-11, and they were in it. The weird thing about their dreams was that they always saw a strange black figure standing on the top of the South Tower screaming at the top of it's lungs. The girls didn't think that it was an ordinary dream so they decided to go back to the building they time traveled with the last time. So they did.

This time when they returned to the building that they haven't been to in 5 years it looked as if it was tortured. They still tried to go in there though, but the door wouldn't open. So Shylynn figured that if they dreamed about it again they could find the building in their dream and get transported in their dream. Gillian thought that was a brilliant idea.

The girls left carrying equipment that they brought just to be more prepared. Now all they have to do now is go to sleep and dream. So the girls ran as fast as they could so they can get tired so they can sleep. Once they got to their home the girls quickly ran into their bedrooms to go to sleep. Then they started to dream.

When they finally got into their dream they found the building and they quietly shut the door.

The girls were amazed by what they saw. What did they see? , you ask. They saw the black figure once again, but that was not all, they saw Anna Lee. What was Anna Lee doing? , you ask. Anna Lee was quickly trying to push the black figure off the South Tower.

Then suddenly the girls looked up to see Anna Lee staring right at the girls. The girls saw the anger in her eyes so the girls decided to run to the top of the tower to make her stop what she was doing. They ran up to them both and yelled,

"STOP!" They both looked at the girls as if they were nuts.

"Why are you here?"
Anna lee asked, "and who are you". The girls were confused. "Don't you know who we are"?

"NO" she yelled. "That's why I asked," she said. The girls answered the question "Well I'm Shylynn and this is Gillian, remember we gave you that note?, but before you answer that question who are you killing?

"I'm Josh I worked here until I got fired and you are probably wondering why I'm so dark, well I was born dark since my whole family is evil and since we're evil, I'm dark.

"Ok then Anna Lee tell us why you want to kill him, said Gillian.

"HE IS TRYING TO DESTROY THE TWIN TOWERS", yelled Anna Lee.

"THAT'S WRONG! yelled the dark figure. I would never do such a thing and how can you prove I'm doing this," the dark figure said.

"Ok, well I overheard my mom talking about it to my grandmother,she said that a man named Josh was going to destroy the twin towers

"Ok then how did you know this?"asked Shylynn.

" She said that she overheard him at the market(grocery store) that he was going to" said Anna Lee.

"Then who was he talking to" asked Gillian.

"Probably to one of his friends" answered Anna Lee.

"Alright Josh you need to end this now" said Gillian.

" Well guess what" said Josh "I can't!, It's all over.

"And when he said that the South tower was demolished. Luckly the girls woke up safe and sound , but they don't have a clue what happened to Anna Lee and Josh. But the one question that they asked Anna Lee was remained a mystery. The girls haven't seen a suspicious girl neither have the had any dreams like the one they had before.

Now that they are older they each have a family. But one thing they can't figure out is that Shylynn's children and Gillian's came to them and said "WE TIME TRAVELED AND SAW 9- 11!

Acknowledgements

Students' Successes Guided by:

Carolyn Armento
Special Class with Integration Teacher
MA, Truman University
BA, Truman University

Becky Baker
Teacher Associate: Special Class
with Integration

Kris Bartz
Full Inclusion Resource Teacher
BA, Central Michigan University
BA, Western Illinois University

Linda Clatt
Teacher Associate: Full Inclusion
Resource

Wendy Boeding
5th Grade General Education Teacher
National Board Certified Teacher
MA, Viterbo University
BA, University of Northern Iowa

Megan Kruse
5th Grade General Education Teacher
National Board Certified Teacher
MA, Viterbo University
BA, University of Northern Iowa

TO ORDER COPIES OF:

Ghost Stories for Kids By Kids

Please send me _____ copies at $9.95 each plus $3.00 S/H each. (Make checks payable to **Quixote Press**.)

Name _____

Street _____

City _____ State ____ Zip _____

Send Orders to:

Quixote Press

3544 Blakslee Street

Wever, IA 52658

800-571-2665

TO ORDER COPIES OF:

Ghost Stories for Kids By Kids

Please send me _____ copies at $9.95 each plus $3.00 S/H each. (Make checks payable to **Quixote Press**.)

Name _____

Street _____

City _____ State ____ Zip _____

Send Orders to:

Quixote Press

3544 Blakslee Street

Wever, IA 52658

800-571-2665